F
CTW
SESAME STREET
G
CTW
SESAME STREET
D
CTW
SESAME STREET
A
K
£5.99

CTW

SESAME STREET®

The Official Annual

Cover illustration: Bruce McNally

Published by Grandreams Limited
435-437 Edgware Road, Little Venice, London W2 1TH

Printed in Belgium

Contents

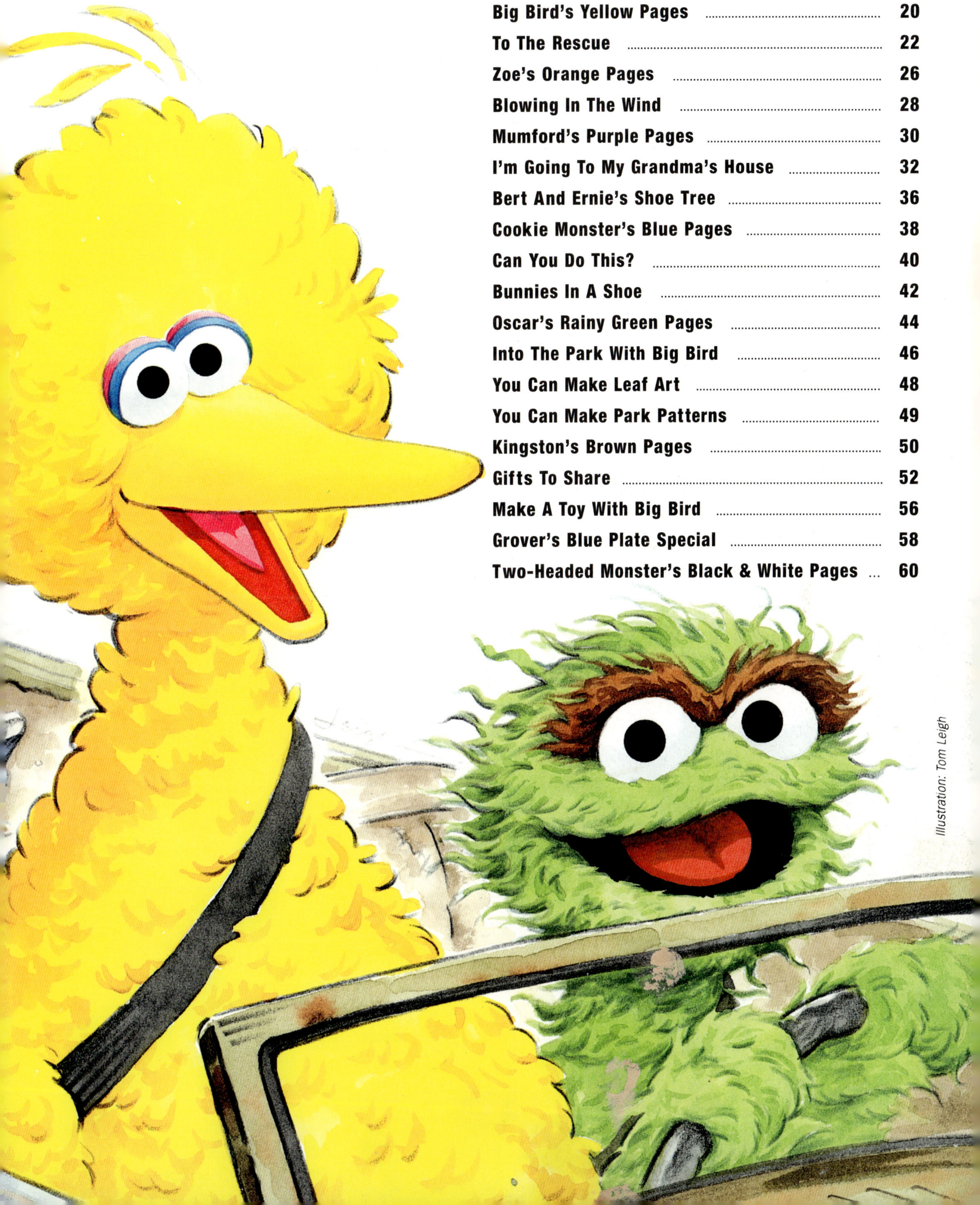

Illustration: Tom Leigh

Hello, and welcome to...

SESAME STREET®

Illustration: Maggie Swanson

We hope you enjoy our new Annual, which is packed with all sorts of fun activities, puzzles and stories! But before you turn the page, take a good look at this picture of all your Sesame Street friends. How many people can you name?

Healthy Food

Bert can't find any fruits and vegetables. He wants to eat them to get the strength and energy he needs to exercise. But Ernie put away the groceries in the wrong places.

Can you help Bert to find the foods pictured below?

watermelon

carrots

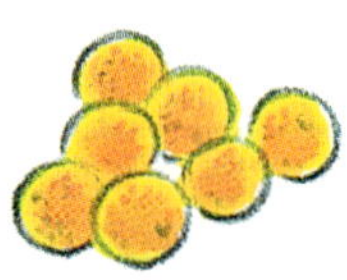

oranges

broccoli

bananas

Illustrations: Tom Brannon

MILK

I'M HAPPY TO BE ME

Illustration: Tom Brannon

④ Finally, Natasha was ready for bed. "Good night, Natasha," Humphrey said. As he was about to turn off the light, Natasha asked, "Ree-ree-ree?"

⑤ "Ingrid," called Humphrey, "what does she mean by 'Ree-ree-ree'?" Natasha repeated her plea, "Ree-ree-ree?" and pointed to the end of the room. "Let her show us," said Ingrid.

⑥ Humphrey put Natasha down on the floor and she crawled to the bookcase. Humphrey and Ingrid soon knew what "Ree-ree-ree" meant. Natasha wanted to be read to!

⑦ Humphrey read from the book Natasha picked. Natasha liked it very much. Soon she fell asleep. What do you think Humphrey read? Turn to the next page to read it, too.

Sleepy Chickies

Little chickies play all day;
Hide and seek and run away!

Then their games and noisy cheeps
Turn to quiet, lazy peeps.

Mother Hen soon comes around –
Time for chicks to settle down.

"Cluck, cluck, cluck!" sweet Mummy cries;
Chickies yawn and rub their eyes.

To the barn they make a path,
And splash like fish inside their bath.

Water cleans their fluffy wings;
Out they hop – soft, yellow things.

Chickies crawl into their nest
And, with their tired mummy, rest.

Happy chickies! Happy hen!
Tomorrow starts the fun again!

Illustration: Lulu Delacre

TELLY'S PINK PAGES

Pink is my favourite colour. I like it because I like pigs and flowers and my fur.

What things can you name that are pink?

Illustration: Sally Vitsky

bow

flower

pig

ice-cream cone

crayon

Draw something pink here or on another piece of paper.
Write its name.

THE COUNT'S OCEAN SAFARI

Dive into the ocean
With my bat friends and me.
Let's look for fun creatures
Who live in the sea.

One clam sits, mouth open;
Two dolphins play tag;
Three starfish are gripping
A steamy rock crag.

A shoal of four blue fish
Swim by in a flash!
Five crabs play and waddle
In dark green sea grass.

It's nice that we've spied them,
But there's more to my plan.
Let's count these sea creatures.
Please start with the clam.

Illustrations: Brad McMahon / Eddie Young

McMAHON

BIG BIRD'S YELLOW PAGES

Hi, girls and boys! Can you find the duckling? What sound does a duck make? *Quack! Quack!*

Do you know anyone who rides in a school bus?

Illustration: Sally Vitsky

my feathers

duckling

shoal of fish

school bus

grapefruit

sun

Draw something yellow here or on another piece of paper. Write its name.

To The Rescue

by Oscar the Grouch

Illustrations: Joe Ewers

1 **I was** making a tuna milk shake when the phone rang. It was Slimey calling from the park. He was trapped in his cousin Rachel's wormhole!

2 **Something** had rolled into the wormhole. It was too heavy to move. I realised I would have to go to the park to help. Grouches don't like parks.

3 **Rachel's** wormhole was near a big tree full of disgusting songbirds. And there were flowers all over the place. Yuck! Luckily, I smelled something wonderful.

4 **It was** a rotten old lump of cheese that someone had thrown onto the ground. I picked up the cheese lump to put it in my can, where garbage belongs. And guess what?

Turn the page

5 **Out** popped Slimey and Rachel! The smelly cheese lump had been blocking Rachel's wormhole.

6 **They** hugged me and said, "Thank you." I said, "Scram!" which is sort of my Grouch way of saying "You're welcome."

7

Listen up, kiddies! Throw your garbage in a can. Hey, throw it in my can. That way, I won't have to go into the park for any more smelly lumps of cheese.

THE END

ZOE'S ORANGE PAGES

Hi! I'm Zoe. Don't tease me! Someone played a Halloween trick and turned the pumpkin white. Can you colour the pumpkin orange?

The word orange is also the name of a fruit.

Illustration: Sally Vitsky

carrots

basketball

tiger

orange

pumpkin

Draw something orange here or on another piece of paper. Write its name.

Blowing in

What's different and what's the same in these two pictures?

the Wind

Illustration: Ellen Appleby

Ask a grown-up for some objects of various shapes and weights – a tissue, a crayon, a ball, and so on. Try to blow each off your hand. What happened?

MUMFORD'S PURPLE PAGES

I, the amazing Mumford, was eating a bunch of grapes when... ***Whoosh!*** My whole lunch turned purple!

What is your favourite colour?
Why do you like that colour?
What things can you name that are your favourite colour?

Illustration: Sally Vitsky

sandwich

banana

Draw something purple here or on another piece of paper. Write its name.

I'm going to my Grandma's house

by Big Bird

I hopped upon my **pogo stick** and bounced down the street; I'm bouncing to my Grandma's house –

Boing, Boing, Boing!

Read the story with a grown up. Then do the actions and make the sounds as you read the story again and again.

At the end of the street, I got aboard a **train**; I'm riding to my Grandma's house –

Woo,

Woo,

Woo!

At the end of the track, I got into a **car**; I'm driving to my Grandma's house –

Beep,

Beep,

Beep!

Turn the page

At the end of the road, I got aboard a **plane**; I'm flying to my Grandma's house –

Zoom,

Zoom,

Zoom!

At the end of the flight, I got into a **boat**; I'm sailing to my Grandma's house –

Whoosh,

Whoosh,

Whoosh!

At the end of the dock, I got onto my **feet**; I'm running to my Grandma's house –
Huff,
Huff,
Huff!

At the end of the trail, I sat on Granny's **porch**; I'm glad I'm at my Grandma's house –
Hmmm,
Hmmm,
Hmmm!
(Good night!)

THE END

Bert and Ernie's

Shoe Tree

Help Bert and Ernie find their shoes. Use your finger and then your crayon to show them the way from START to STOP

What's funny about this picture? What do you usually see growing on trees?

Illustration: Tommy Stubbs

STOP

COOKIE MONSTER'S BLUE PAGES

Hello. Cookie Monster here. Me like the colour blue and me like to eat blueberries. What things do *you* like that are blue?

How many blue things are on these pages? Count me too! Write the number:

blue jays

Illustration: Sally Vitsky

Cookie Monster's lunch box

lollipops

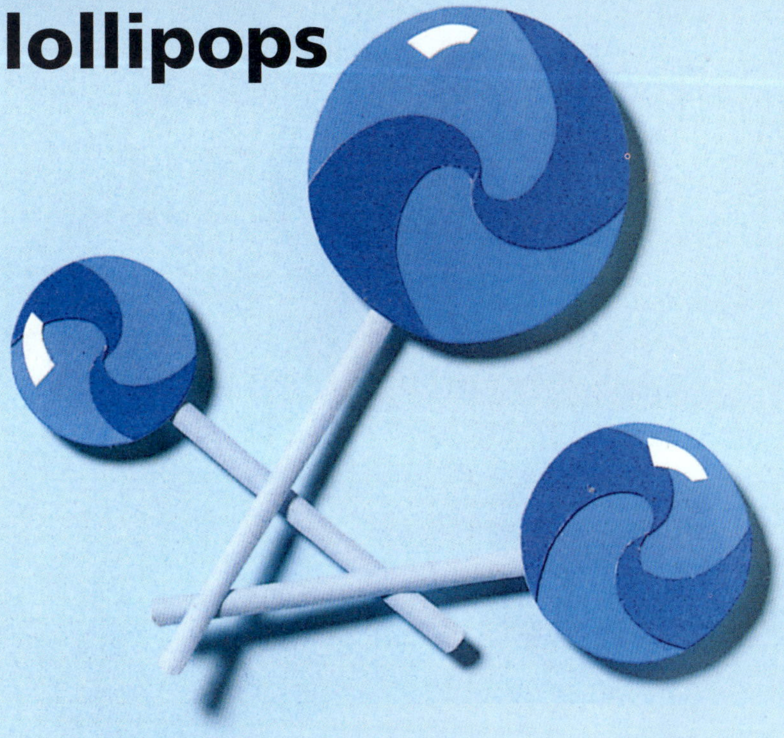

blueberries

Draw something blue here or on another piece of paper. Write its name.

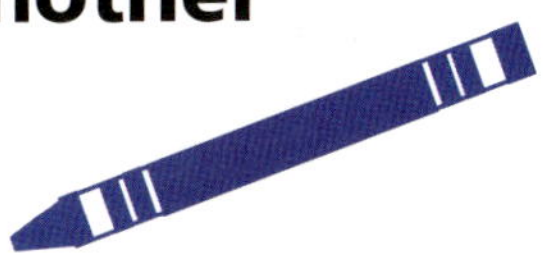

Can You Do This?

Can you hop like a frog?

Photography: Dennis Mosner

Can you touch your nose with your tongue?
Can you jump with your arms up high?
Can you balance a book on your head?
Can you rub your tummy and pat your head at the same time?

CTW SESAME STREET®

Gallery

BUNNIES IN A SHOE

There once was a rabbit,
Who lived in a shoe.
She had so many bunnies,
She didn't know what to do.

How many little bunnies does Mummy rabbit have?

Illustration: Lawrence DiFiori

1 2 3 4 5 6 7 8 9 10 11 12 13 14

15 16 17 18 19 20 21 22 23 24 25

OSCAR'S RAINY GREEN PAGES

YUCK, I don't like spring. But I love the muddy and messy rain! It helps things grow that are the same colour as me – green.

Which of these green things do you think Oscar likes? Count the green things here. Write the number:

leaf

peas

broccoli

frog

Illustration: Sally Vitsky / David Dees

grasshopper

stinkweed

Draw something green here or on another piece of paper. Write its name.

Into the Park with Big Bird

I walked in the park
– what a wonderful day!
You can see what I saw,
if you do as I say:

Find me some kids
Who are spinning around.
Find me a critter
That lives underground.

Find me a kite
Floating high as a cloud.
Find me a girl
Playing ball; she's so proud!

Find me a horse
In a big wooden shed.
Find me Bert's bird;
See her pecking for bread?

Find me a friend
Painting two chirping birds.
Find me the bird
Who is writing these words!

Illustration: Joe Mathieu

RECYCLE

You Can Make
Leaf Art

What you need

- Leaves that have fallen from trees
- Tape or paste
- Paper
- Crayons

What you do

1. Tape or paste the leaves to the paper.
2. Draw a picture around each leaf.
3. Hang up your leaf art where everyone can see it.

Illustration: Katherine Osbourne

You Can Make Park Patterns

What is missing in each row? Point to the picture that shows it below. Or draw it in the box at the end of the row.

How many red leaves are there? Write the number here.

Count *all* the flowers!

Illustration: Paul Richer

KINGSTON'S BROWN PAGES

Hello, I'm Kingston Livingston III. I like the colour brown. I took a trip to the zoo and saw all these brown animals. Can you name them?

With what letter do all these animals' names begin? Write some B's here:

Illustration: Sally Vitsky

bear

beetle

beaver

bat

bird

Draw something brown here or on another piece of paper. Write its name.

Gifts to Share

Illustration: Joe Ewers

Elmo held his broken train set. Big Bird had a stuffed tiger with a torn tail. They were taking their old toys to the Fix-It Shop.

"Maria and Luis will fix our toys and send them to little monsters who don't have any," said Big Bird.

"Elmo thinks that will make the monsters very happy," said Elmo.

On the way to the shop, Big Bird and Elmo met Zoe and Rosita. Elmo told them about giving away old toys. Zoe and Rosita thought that was nice.

"I have a broken tambourine," said Rosita. "And I have an old trumpet," said Zoe.

Turn the page

"Bring them along," said Big Bird. He led them to Oscar's trash can. The cranky Grouch popped out.

"Do you have any broken toys?" Big Bird asked.

"Yes, I do, beak-face!" Oscar said. "Stop buggin' me and I'll get 'em."

Oscar, Big Bird, and the monsters arrived at the Fix-It Shop.

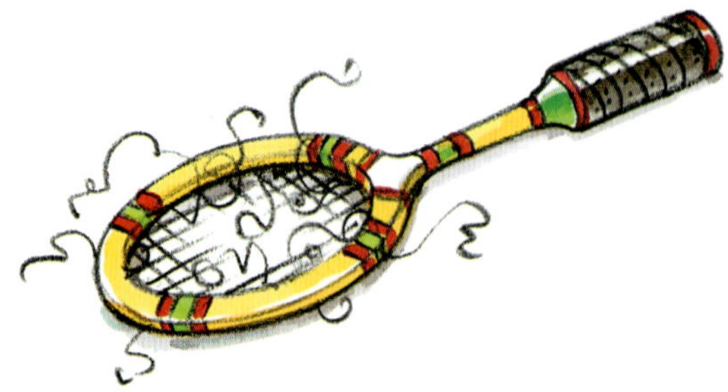

"Thanks for giving up your old toys," said Maria. "There are so many!"

"How will we fix them in time?" said Luis.

"*We* could help you fix the toys!" said Big Bird.
"We could be your helper elves!" Elmo chimed in.
Everyone laughed at the thought of being elves.
"Great idea!" said Maria. "Let's get to work."

THE END

Make A Toy With Big Bird

1. Use a crayon to colour the truck.

2. You can draw something that rolls on wheels on the next page.

Illustration: David Dees

This toy was made by

(Write your name here.)

GROVER'S
BLUE
CAFÉ
BLUES BROTHERS

Illustration: Ellen Appleby

Grover's Blue Plate Special

Hello.

It is I, your cute and furry little monster, Grover. Welcome to my Blue Café, where many things are blue – even the food. Unfortunately, some of my guests complain that too many things are blue.

What things in the picture should stay blue? What would you like to change? Please tell me, because at Grover's Blue Café, the customer is always right!

Two-Headed Monster's Black & White Pages

The Two-Headed Monster likes black and it also likes white. Point to the black crow. Touch the white snowflakes. Which pictures are both black and white?

Can you find items in your house that are black, white, or both black and white?

Illustration: Sally Vitsky

snowflakes

penguin

piano

crow

book

Draw something black, white, or both black and white – here or on another piece of paper. Write its name.

A
CTW
SESAME STREET
S
C
CTW
SESAME STREET
H
CTW
SESAME STREET